IMAGINE

RUTH BROWN

Andersen Press • London

Imagine,
when you're half asleep,
those big white clouds
look just like sheep . . .

in a meadow, in the spring.

Just imagine . . . anything!

Imagine slow,

imagine fast,

Imagine first,

imagine last.

Imagine round,

imagine flat,

Imagine thin,

imagine fat.

Imagine short,

imagine long,

Imagine weak,

imagine strong.

Imagine hot,

imagine cold,

Imagine new,

imagine old.

Imagine dark,

imagine light,

And now it's time to sleep.
Goodnight!

Other books by
RUTH BROWN:

The Christmas Mouse
written by Toby Forward

Snail Trail

Ten Seeds

Lion in the Long Grass
illustrated by Ken Brown

Mr Bear and the Bear
written by Frances Thomas

Night-time Tale